Grandmother School

Rina Singh and *Ellen Rooney*

ORCA BOOK PUBLISHERS

"Hurry up, Aaji!" I tell my grandmother.

    I know she doesn't like being late. She rushes through her chores so she can change into her uniform—a bright pink sari. She checks her bag for her abacus, reader, slate and chalk. She looks into the little mirror on the wall and freshens up the red dot on her forehead.

Then I take her hand in mine and walk her to school.

Her school is a one-room bamboo hut at the end of the mango grove. It has a thatched roof, and the mud floor is covered with mats for the grandmothers to sit on. The door is decorated with marigold garlands, and inside there is a big chalkboard. The grandmothers sit in rows, ready to practice the alphabet on their slates and show their work to the teacher.

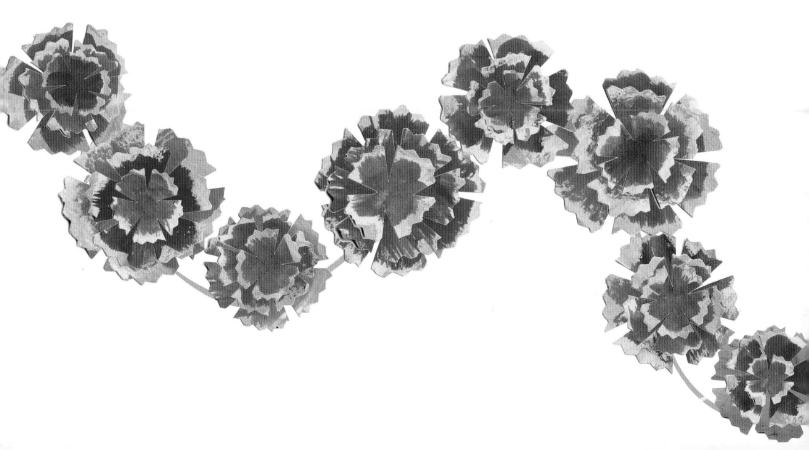

Aaji started school a year ago. My teacher said almost everyone in the village could read, write and count except for all of the grandmothers.
So he built Aajibaichi Shala—Grandmother School.

Ajoba—my grandfather—shook his head and said that learning at this age was a waste of time, but most of the people in the village were happy for the grandmothers.

When Aaji first learned to spell her name, she did a little dance.

Then she went to the bank. The rude man behind the counter had always dismissed her, saying people who give thumbprints instead of signatures have to wait. He made her feel small. "Now I'll show him I can sign my name," she said.

In the evenings we huddle together, share stories and do our homework. When Aaji needs help, she whispers in my ear. She doesn't want anyone to know she's having trouble.

In one year at Aajibaichi Shala, she has learned the alphabet.

She can read and spell many words.

She is so proud that she can even add and subtract.

One day one of the grandmothers fell ill, and the others weren't able to pay attention to the lessons. So the teacher let the grandmothers worry and pray together.

That night Aaji hugged me a little tighter and said, "When I die and my Creator asks me what I did with my life on earth, I'll say I learned to sign my name."

"But, Aaji," I reminded her. "You can also read words like *cloud, sky, rain, tree, mango, water, bird, hill, river...*"

"Yes, and I'll take all those words with me to the next world."

On days when Aaji falls asleep before me, I can hear her chanting rhymes in her sleep, the ones the teacher has asked her to memorize.

I am so proud of her.

Most days, after the evening meal, she tells me
stories before I sleep. My favorites are about the
warrior king who was brave, kind and clever. The king,
Shivaji, was courageous and won many daring battles,
but he never hurt those he didn't need to.

I especially love the story where King Shivaji escaped from a prison by hiding in a large fruit basket, outwitting Aurangzeb, the cruelest emperor that ever ruled India.

No matter what story she is sharing, Aaji always ends with the same line. "One day I will read you this story from a book."

पाऊस

झाड ८

४ ६

प्रेम

But not tonight. Tonight I have already
drifted into sleep, dreaming of warriors and
birds, numbers and words.

Author's Note

In Phangane, a remote village in India about 77 miles (125 kilometers) from Mumbai, there is a school just for grandmothers, the Aajibaichi Shala. It was the creation of Yogendra Bangar, a local schoolteacher, who wanted everyone in the village to be able to read and write. He built the one-room school and invited Phangane's twenty-nine grandmothers to attend. The students are all over the age of sixty, and the oldest grandmother is ninety.

Some of the women are hard of hearing and some of them forget what they have learned, but they all come, dressed in their bright pink saris. They are excited to learn.

Their grandchildren walk them to school every day except Thursday, which is a prayer day. And for two hours in the afternoon, sitting in the scorching heat, they learn the Marathi alphabet, numbers, nursery rhymes and new words.

As children, these grandmothers watched their brothers go to school. As mothers, they sent their own children to school. But no one gave them a chance to go to school.

In March 2016 they were given a chance, and they took it. Like their warrior king, Shivaji, these courageous grandmothers escaped the prison of illiteracy and no longer endure this shame.

In memory of Biji, my grandmother, who would have loved school.
—R.S.

In memory of Uncle Jimmy.
—E.R.

Text copyright © Rina Singh 2020
Illustrations copyright © Ellen Rooney 2020

Cataloguing in Publication information available from Library and Archives Canada
Title: Grandmother school / Rina Singh and [illustrated by] Ellen Rooney.
Names: Singh, Rina, 1955– author. | Rooney, Ellen, illustrator.
Identifiers: Canadiana (print) 20190224614 | Canadiana (ebook) 20190224916 | ISBN 9781459819054 (hardcover) | ISBN 9781459819061 (PDF) | ISBN 9781459819078 (EPUB)
Subjects: LCSH: Aajibaichi Shala—Juvenile literature. | LCSH: Older women—Education—Juvenile literature.
Classification: LCC LC5493.12 P53 2020 | DDC j371.824/6—DC23

Library of Congress Control Number: 2019954269
Simultaneously published in Canada and the United States in 2020

Summary: This brilliantly illustrated picture book tells the story of the Aajibaichi Shala, the Grandmother School, that was opened in Phangane, India, in 2016 to teach local grandmothers how to read and write.

Orca Book Publishers is committed to reducing the consumption of nonrenewable resources in the making of our books. We make every effort to use materials that support a sustainable future.

Orca Book Publishers gratefully acknowledges the support for its publishing programs provided by the following agencies: the Government of Canada, the Canada Council for the Arts and the Province of British Columbia through the BC Arts Council and the Book Publishing Tax Credit.

The illustrations were rendered with a variety of materials, including pencils, acrylic paints, gouache, hand-carved stamps and digital drawing tools.

Cover and interior artwork by Ellen Rooney
Edited by Liz Kemp
Design by Rachel Page

ORCA BOOK PUBLISHERS
orcabook.com

Printed and bound in China.

23 22 21 20 • 4 3 2 1

Rina Singh has published several critically acclaimed books for children inspired by her Indian Canadian heritage, including *Diwali Lights, Holi Colors* and *Diwali: A Festival of Lights*, which was nominated for the Red Cedar Award. Rina's own grandmother never got the chance to go to school. *Grandmother School* is dedicated to her memory. Rina lives in Toronto with her family.

Ellen Rooney is a designer, artist and children's book illustrator. Her textural mixed media artwork combines many traditional art techniques, like pencil drawing, painting, printmaking and collage, often combined with digital techniques. Originally from Massachusetts, she now lives in the southern Okanagan Valley in British Columbia.